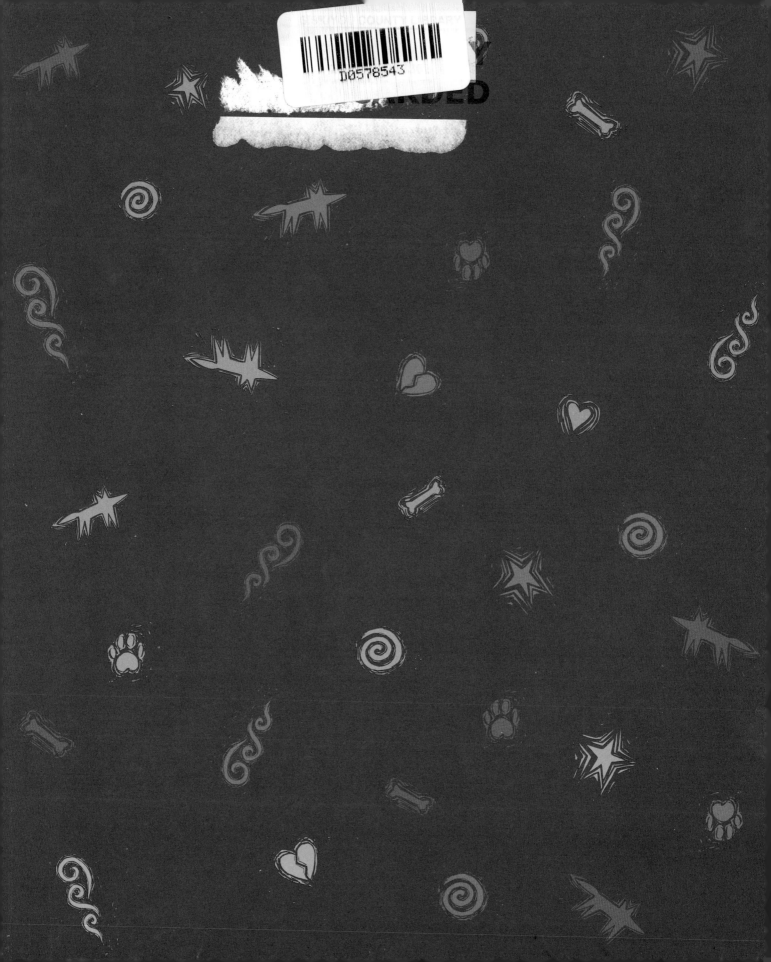

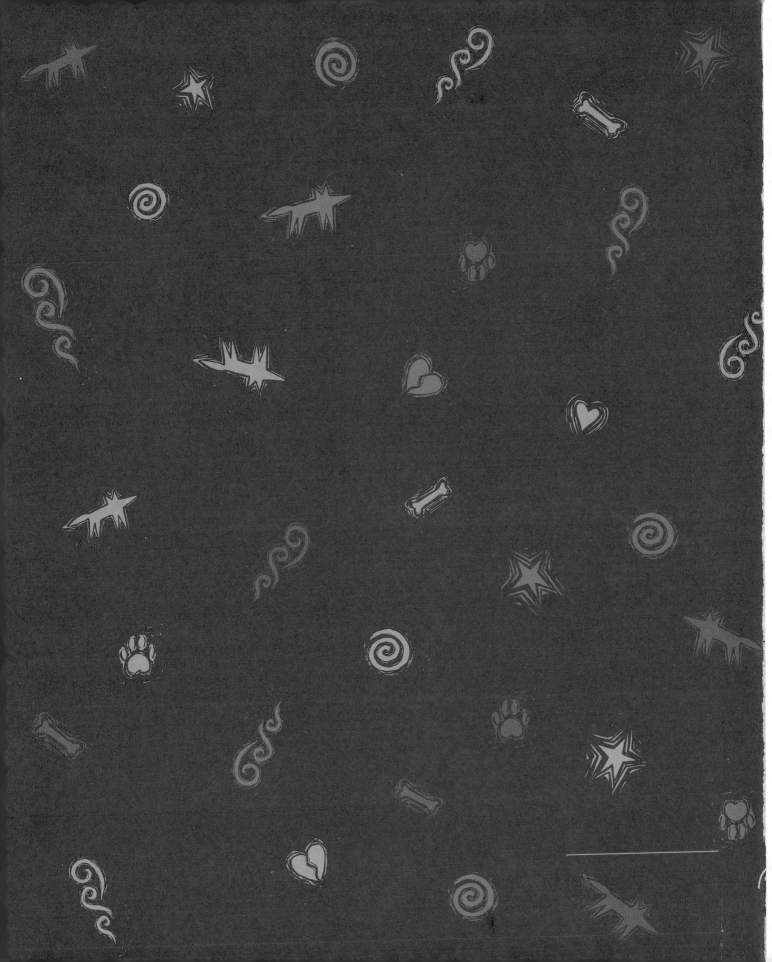

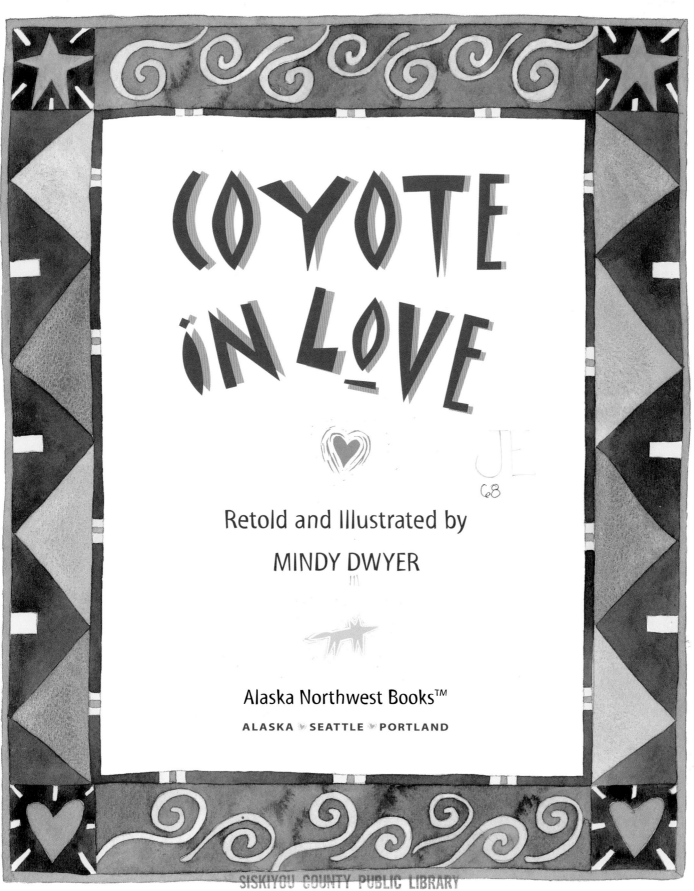

COYOTE IN LOVE

Retold and Illustrated by

MINDY DWYER

Alaska Northwest Books™

ALASKA ❤ SEATTLE ❤ PORTLAND

This is an old tale of love and the way things came to be ★★★★

BACK IN THE OLD DAYS, when the world was changing, Coyote had magical powers. It was his job to put things in order. This is what the Old Ones believed.

But Coyote was
ALWAYS

GETTING INTO TROUBLE.

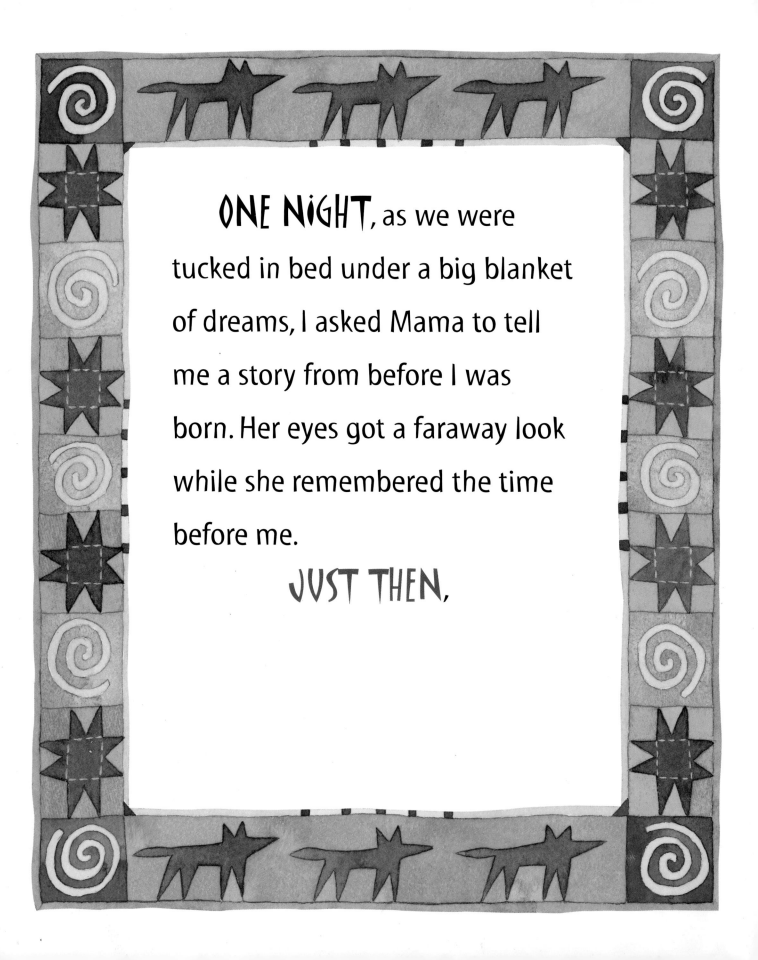

ONE NIGHT, as we were tucked in bed under a big blanket of dreams, I asked Mama to tell me a story from before I was born. Her eyes got a faraway look while she remembered the time before me.

JUST THEN,

a band of coyotes SANGᵍᵍᵍᵍᵍᵍ

outside our window.

Mama smiled and began to speak

in a voice as soft and

magical as the

twinkly edges

of a star.

A LONG TIME AGO,

she said, when the world was still very new, Coyote liked to sit and look at stars. He would stay up all night, watching the stars fade into the pink light that brought morning. There was one star that was his favorite and he found her more beautiful than any other star in the sky. Coyote was **IN LOVE** with her.

SHE was a BLUE star, and each night Coyote sat and waited until she appeared. As he watched her blue glow travel across the night sky, he sang to her.

He noticed she always came very close to the tip of a distant mountain. "If I go to the TOP of that mountain, I could touch her!"

Coyote started to *run* across the fields and into the forest. He *ran* and *ran* and *ran*

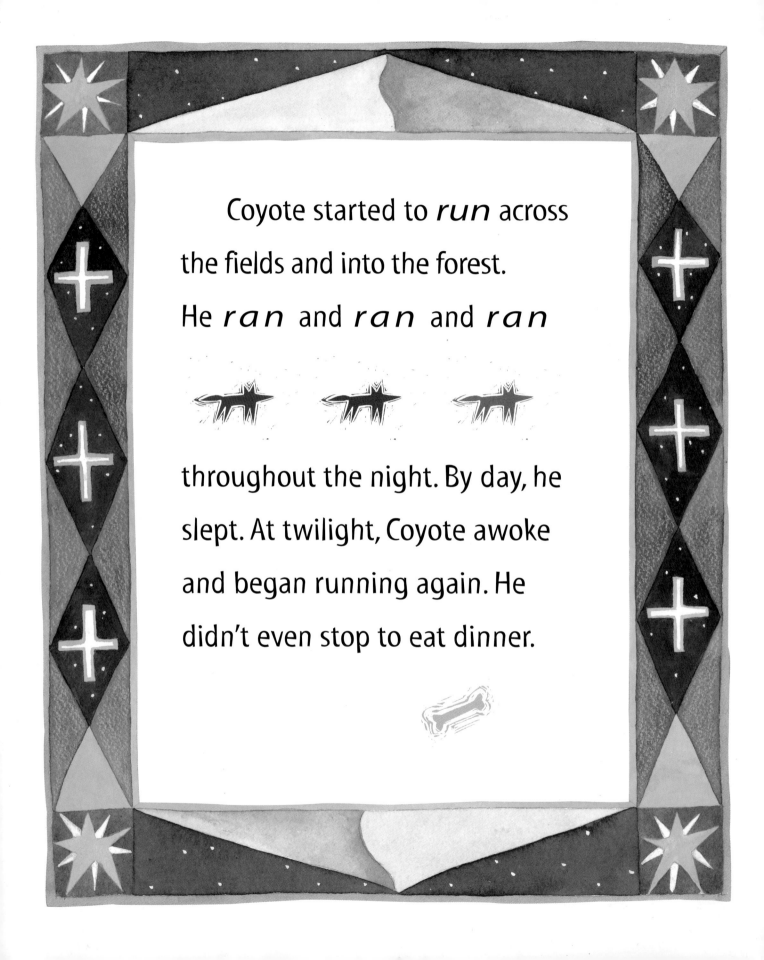

throughout the night. By day, he slept. At twilight, Coyote awoke and began running again. He didn't even stop to eat dinner.

HE climbed and climbed until **AT LAST** he reached the top of the mountain.

There he watched the sunset, freshly painted in the sky. The colors melted and dripped behind the edge of the earth, and their soft afterglow soothed him. Coyote was v e r y   t i r e d, but he didn't want to miss his BEAUTIFUL star.

ONE by ONE the stars began to show their shining night faces. With nothing but sky all around him, Coyote could see the stars twinkling. But NO ...

THEY WERE DANCING. For a moment he thought he was dreaming. He blinked. Suddenly, he saw her—his little blue star—and she was

RADIANT!

COYOTE stood up on top of the mountain and stretched, but still he could not reach her. Politely, he said, "My little star, take me with you. I LOVE YOU. I want you to be my wife."

The little star said, "HA! I don't want to be your wife!"

Coyote begged. "PLEEEEASE!"

THEN Coyote leaped up and GRABBED her.

But she was a sky being and did not like being grabbed one bit. The little star scolded him:

"OH, YOU ARE A SILLY COYOTE!"

She held him by the paws and PULLED Coyote into the sky, higher and higher through the clouds.

HE was ☺ dizzzzy ☺ with love and afraid to look down. The little star took Coyote to the edge of the sky, where it was so dark and quiet it chilled him to the bone.

"I'm scared," he said.

"i

FEEL

LiKE

i'M

FALLLLLiNG."

The blue star said, "Coyote, YOU ARE SUCH A FOOL," and let him go. Coyote fell, tumbling through the starry cover of night.

Then Mama asked us, "Can you hear Coyote falling?" We YELLLPED like little coyote pups as we imagined him plunging through the sky. "YIP, YIP,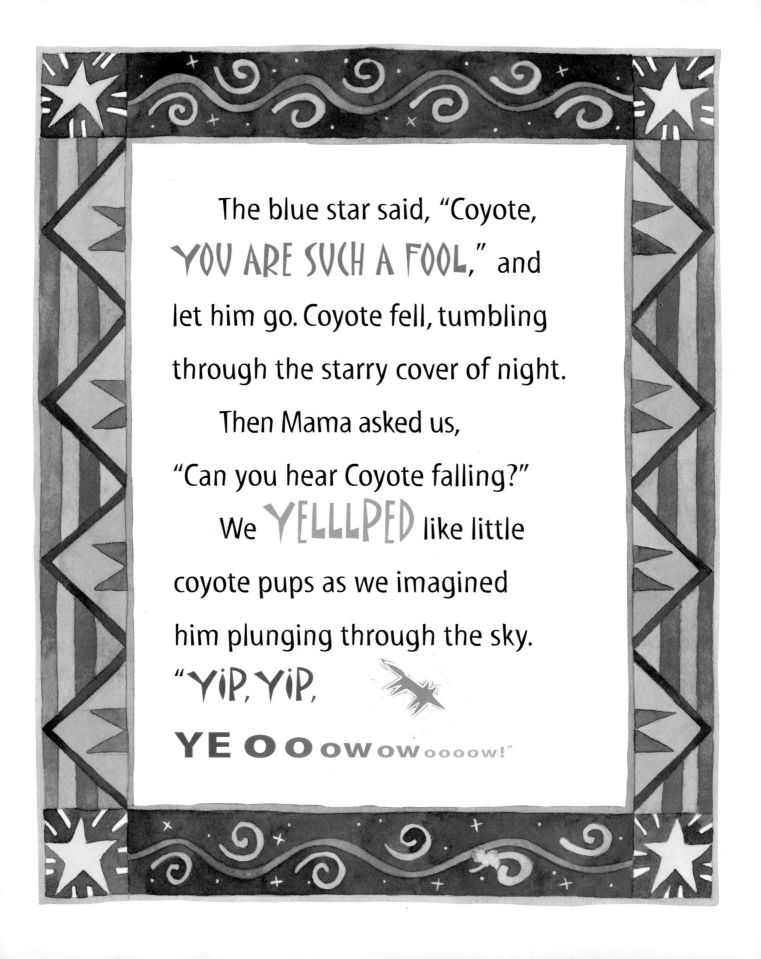

YE O O OW OW ooow!"

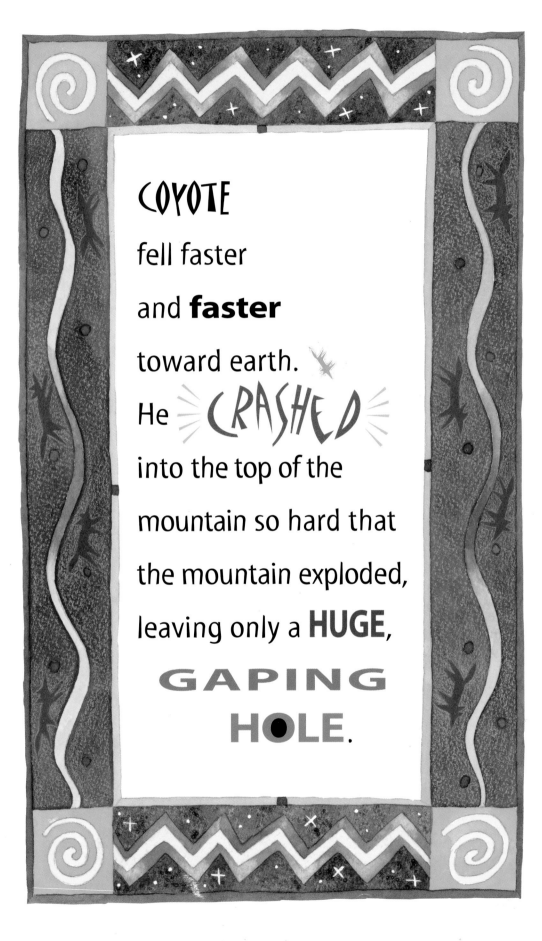

COYOTE
fell faster
and **faster**
toward earth.
He CRASHED
into the top of the
mountain so hard that
the mountain exploded,
leaving only a **HUGE**,
GAPING
HOLE.

COYOTE cried and cried. His heart was broken. Where he had touched the star, Coyote's paws were **BLUE**, and the tears he cried were blue, too.

Soon **COYOTE'S** tears filled the great hole in the mountaintop, making a clear blue lake. Today we call it **CRATER LAKE**. And now you know how Crater Lake came to be and why the lake is

SO BLUE
even
to
this
VERY
day.

Have **YOU** ever heard a
coyote singing on a starry night?
Could it be the song of
COYOTE IN LOVE?